George Peele's The Old Wives' Tale: A Retelling

David Bruce

Published by David Bruce, 2022.

This is a work of fiction. Similarities to real people, places, or events are entirely coincidental.

GEORGE PEELE'S THE OLD WIVES' TALE: A RETELLING

First edition. July 20, 2022.

Copyright © 2022 David Bruce.

ISBN: 979-8201582555

Written by David Bruce.

Table of Contents

Dedication

Dedicated to Carl Eugene Bruce and Josephine Saturday Bruce

My father, Carl Eugene Bruce, died on 24 October 2013. He used to work for Ohio Power, and at one time, his job was to shut off the electricity of people who had not paid their bills. He sometimes would find a home with an impoverished mother and some children. Instead of shutting off their electricity, he would tell the mother that she needed to pay her bill or soon her electricity would be shut off. He would write on a form that no one was home when he stopped by because if no one was home he did not have to shut off their electricity.

The best good deed that anyone ever did for my father occurred after a storm that knocked down many power lines. He and other linemen worked long hours and got wet and cold. Their feet were freezing because water got into their boots and soaked their socks. Fortunately, a kind woman gave my father and the other linemen dry socks to wear.

My mother, Josephine Saturday Bruce, died on 14 June 2003. She used to work at a store that sold clothing. One day, an impoverished mother with a baby clothed in rags walked into the store and started shoplifting in an interesting way: The mother took the rags off her baby and dressed the infant in new clothing. My mother knew that this mother could not afford to buy the clothing, but she helped the mother dress her baby and then she watched as the mother walked out of the store without paying.

My mother and my father both died at 7:40 p.m.

Cover Photograph for George Peele's *The Old Wives' Tale*: A Retelling:

Victoria Borodinova

https://pixabay.com/en/story-fairy-forest-magic-sorceress-2972523/

Educate Yourself
Read Like A Wolf Eats
Be Excellent to Each Other
Books Then, Books Now, Books Forever

***

In this retelling, as in all my retellings, I have tried to make the work of literature accessible to modern readers who may lack some of the knowledge about mythology, religion, and history that the literary work's contemporary audience had.

Do you know a language other than English? If you do, I give you permission to translate this book, copyright your translation, publish or self-publish it, and keep all the royalties for yourself. (Do give me credit, of course, for the original retelling.)

I would like to see my retellings of classic literature used in schools, so I give permission to the country of Finland (and all other countries) to give copies of this book to all students forever. I also give permission to the state of Texas (and all other states) to give copies of this book to all students forever. I also give permission to all teachers to give copies of this book to all students forever.

Teachers need not actually teach my retellings. Teachers are welcome to give students copies of my books as background material. For example, if they are teaching Homer's *Iliad* and *Odyssey*, teachers are welcome to give students copies of my *Virgil's* Aeneid: *A Retelling in Prose* and tell students, "Here's another ancient epic you may want to read in your spare time."

CAST OF CHARACTERS

Contemporary Characters:

Antic. A Servant. An antic person is a ludicrous person.

Frolic. A Servant. A frolicsome person is a merry, playful person.

Fantastic. A Servant. A fantastic person is a fanciful person.

Clunch. A Blacksmith.

Madge. His Wife. She is an old woman whom others call "gammer," which means "grandmother."

***

Fairy Tale Characters:

Sacrapant. An evil Conjuror.

First Brother, named Calypha. A Prince. He is Delia's brother.

Second Brother, named Thelea. A Prince. He is Delia's brother.

Delia. Sister to Calypha and Thelea. She is a Princess.

Eumenides. A Wandering Knight. In love with Delia.

Huanebango. A Braggart Knight.

Booby. A Clown. Huanebango's companion.

Erestus. A benevolent old man who keeps (dwells at) the cross. The cross in an intersection that is marked by a cross.

Venelia. Betrothed to Erestus, the benevolent old man.

Lampriscus. Neighbor to Erestus.

Zantippa. Daughter to Lampriscus by his first wife. She is pretty, but she is also shrewish and argumentative.

Celanta. Daughter to Lampriscus by his second wife. She is an ugly wench, but she is not shrewish.

Wiggen. Friend to Jack.

Corebus. Friend to Jack.

Ghost of Jack. A deceased person.

Churchwarden, named Steven Loach. The word "loach" means "idiot." A churchwarden makes sure the church buildings and grounds are taken care of.

Sexton. A sexton digs graves and looks after church grounds.

Hostess. Worker at an inn.

***

Minor Characters:

Friar, Harvestmen and Harvestwomen, two Furies, Fiddlers, etc.

***

NOTES:

Characters in early Elizabethan plays often refer to themselves in the third person.

The original play was published without scene divisions. Different editors divide the play into different numbers of scenes.

In this culture, a person of higher rank would use words such as "thee," "thy," "thine," and "thou" to refer to a servant. However, two close friends or a husband and wife could properly use "thee," "thy," "thine," and "thou" to refer to each other.

Some editions call Booby the Clown by the name "Booby" before switching to the name "Corebus." Another character is named "Corebus" — this seems to be a different Corebus than Booby, so this book uses the name "Booby" consistently for the Clown.

The word "Eumenides" — the name of the good wandering knight — means "The Kindly Ones." In Aeschylus' *Oresteia*, the Furies are spirits of vengeance, but in the third play of the trilogy, they become spirits who protect justice and are renamed the Eumenides.

The word "wench" need not necessarily have a negative connotation. In this book, it is often used affectionately.

Zantippa is a shrewish woman. The ancient philosopher Socrates' wife, Xantippe, was reputed to be shrewish.

CHAPTER 1

— Scene 1 —

Antic, Frolic, and Fantastic, all of whom were young male servants to a lovesick master, were lost in the woods of England at night.

"How are you now, fellow Frolic!" Antic said. "All downcast and dejected? Does this sadness become thy madcapness? So what if we have lost our way in the woods? Don't hang your head as though thou have no hope to live until tomorrow, for Fantastic and I will guarantee thy life tonight for twenty in the hundred."

Antic was saying that he and Fantastic would offer 5-to-1 odds that Frolic would not die this night.

"Antic and Fantastic, as I am a frolicsome, merry, gay fellow, never in all my life was I slain so dead — I am practically already frightened to death and exhausted!" Frolic replied. "To lose our way in the wood, without either fire or candle, and to be so uncomfortable! Oh, *coelum*! Oh, *terra*! Oh, *maria*! Oh, Neptune!

The Latin words meant "Oh, heaven! Oh, land! Oh, seas!"

"Oh, Maria!" can also mean "Oh, Mary!" Mary is the Virgin Mary.

Neptune is the Roman name of the god of the sea.

"Why are thou acting so strange and carrying on like that, seeing Cupid has led our young master to the fair lady, and she is the only saint whom he has sworn to serve?" Fantastic said. "Our young master is in love with the beautiful lady."

"What is left for us to do, then, but to entrust him to his wench, and each of us climb and take his stand up in a tree, and sing out our bad luck to the popular tune of 'Oh, Man in Desperation'?" Frolic asked.

Frolic used the word "wench" affectionately.

"Desperately spoken, fellow Frolic, in the dark," Antic said, "but seeing that things turned out this way, let us recite the old proverb:

"*Three merry men, and three merry men,*

"*And three merry men be we:*

"*I in the wood, and thou on the ground,*

"*And Jack sleeps in the tree.*"

A dog barked.

"Hush!" Fantastic said. "A dog in the wood, or a wooden dog!"

He was punning: the word "wood" could mean "insane" or "rabid" or "ferocious," and the word "wooden" could mean "stupid."

"Oh, what a comfortable thing to hear!" he continued, "But I had just as soon that the chamberlain of the White Horse Inn had called me up to bed."

In this society, a chamberlain was the person in charge of the bedrooms at an inn.

Frolic said, "Either this trotting cur — this ambling dog — has gone out of his circuit, or else we are near some village, which should not be far off, for I perceive the glimmering of a firefly, a candle, or a cat's eye, I bet my life against a halfpenny!"

Clunch, a blacksmith carrying a lantern and candle, arrived.

"In the name of my own father, even if you are an ox or ass that appear, tell us who thou are," Frolic said.

"Who am I? Why, I am Clunch the blacksmith. Who are you? What do you make in my territories at this time of the night?"

In this society, "What do you make?" meant "What are you doing?"

"What do we make, do thou ask?" Antic asked. "Why, we make faces out of fear; they are such that, if thy mortal eyes could behold them, would make thee pee down the long sides of thy trousers, blacksmith."

"And, truly, sir, unless your hospitality relieves us, we are likely to continue to wander, with a sorrowful sigh — heigh-ho — among the owlets and hobgoblins of the forest," Frolic said. "Good Vulcan, for Cupid's sake who has tricked us all, befriend us as thou may; and command us howsoever, wheresoever, whensoever, in whatsoever, for ever and ever. We will be in your debt for ever and ever."

Vulcan is the Roman name of the blacksmith god and is therefore a good nickname to call Clunch the blacksmith.

Cupid is the god of love and the son of Venus. Frolic and his fellow servants are lost because of events following their master's falling in love, and so it is appropriate for Frolic to blame Cupid for their plight.

"Well, sirs, it seems to me you have lost your way in the wood," Clunch said, "in consideration whereof, if you will go with Clunch to his cottage, you shall have houseroom and a good fire to sit by, although we have no bedding to put you in."

Antic, Frolic, and Fantastic cried together, "Oh, blessed blacksmith! Oh, generous Clunch!"

"For your further entertainment, it shall be as it may be, and so on," Clunch said. "Things must be as they shall be."

They walked until they reached Clunch's home, where they heard a dog bark.

"Listen!" Clunch said. "This is Ball, my dog, that bids you all welcome in his own language. Come, when you go inside, be careful not to stumble on the threshold — that's bad luck."

He called, "Open the door, Madge; we have guests."

His old wife, Madge, opened the door.

"Welcome, Clunch, and good fellows all, who come with my goodman," Madge said. "For my goodman's sake, come on, sit down. Here is a piece of cheese, and a pudding of my own making."

A pudding is either a sausage or a sweet dish.

In this society, the word "goodman" meant "head of the household"; in this case, it also meant "husband."

"Thanks, gammer," Antic said. "You are a good example for the wives of our town."

In this society, the word "gammer," which meant "grandmother," was used as a nickname for an old woman.

"Gammer, thou and thy goodman sit lovingly together," Frolic said. "We come to chat, and not to eat."

Frolic was polite and did not want to put their hosts to any trouble. And since the blacksmith and his wife were not expecting guests, chances are there was not really enough food to go around.

"Well, sirs, if you will eat nothing, let's clear the table," Clunch said.

He was polite and did not want to eat in front of them.

Clunch then asked, "Come, what will we do to pass away the time?"

He said to his wife, "Lay a crabapple in the fire to roast for lamb's-wool."

Lamb's-wool was a drink made of ale, the pulp of roasted apples, sugar, and spices.

He then asked his guests, "Shall we have a game at trump or ruff to drive away and pass the time? What do you say?"

Trump and ruff are card games.

"This blacksmith leads a life as merry as a king with Madge, his wife," Fantastic said. "Sirrah Frolic, I am sure thou are not without some round or other. I have no doubt that Clunch can bear his part."

In this case, "sirrah" was an affectionate form of address, one friend to another. Neither friend ranked high socially.

A round is a song in which different singers sing various parts, one singer at a time.

"Else you think that I am badly brought up, start the song when you will," Frolic said. "I will sing my part."

They sang:

"*When the rye reach to the chin,*

"*And chopcherry, chopcherry ripe within,*

"*Strawberries swimming in the cream,*

"*And schoolboys playing in the stream;*

"*Then, O, then, O, then, O, my true-love said,*

"*Till that time come again*

"*She could not live [as] a maid.*"

"Chopcherry" is a game in which the player tried to catch in his or her mouth a cherry suspended on a string.

"Maids" are maidens: unmarried women, virgins.

"This entertainment is good," Antic said, "but I think, gammer, that a merry winter's tale would drive away the time trimly and well. Come, I am sure you are not without a score of such merry tales to while away a winter's evening."

"Indeed, gammer," Fantastic said. "A tale of an hour long is as good as an hour's sleep."

"Look, gammer, I am sure you know such tales as that of the giant and the king's daughter, and I know not what else," Frolic said. "I have seen the day, when I was a little one, I would have followed a moving storyteller for a mile so I could hear such a tale."

"Well, since you are so insistent, my goodman shall fill the pot with ale and get him to bed," Madge said. "They who ply their work must keep good hours. One of you, go lie with him."

Her husband had already heard her winter's tales, so it made sense for him to rest so he could work hard the next day.

In this society, it was considered proper for individuals of the same sex to share beds. In winter, sharing a bed helped keep both people warm.

Madge said, "He is a clean-skinned man, I tell you, without either spavin or windgall."

She meant that her husband the blacksmith was healthy and free of disease. His skin was free of sores, and he did not suffer from either spavin or windgall — which are horse diseases!

"Do that, and I am happy to drive away the time with an old wives' winter's tale," she said.

"There's no better hay in Devonshire; on my word, gammer," Fantastic said. "I'll be one of your audience."

A "hay" is a dance. Fantastic was saying that there was no better entertainment in Devonshire than an old wives' winter's tale.

"And I will be another," Frolic said. "That's settled."

"Then I must go to bed with the goodman," Antic said. "*Bona nox*, gammer. God night, Frolic."

"*Bona nox*" is Latin for "good night."

"God night" means "May God give you a good night."

"Come on, my lad," Clunch said. "Thou shall take thy unnatural rest with me."

The rest was unnatural because normally the blacksmith shared the bed with his wife, but the blacksmith was also gently joking that it was unnatural because a mature man and a young man were sharing the same bed.

Antic and the blacksmith exited.

"Yet we shall have this advantage over them in the morning," Frolic said. "We will be ready at the sight of the dawn to leave extempore — no preparation needed because we will have our shoes on."

"Now this agreement, my masters, I must make with you," Madge said. "You will say 'hum' and 'ha' to my tale, so I shall know you are awake."

"Agreed, gammer," Frolic and Fantastic said. "We will do that."

Madge began telling her old wives' winter's tale:

"Once upon a time, there was a king, or a lord, or a duke, who had a beautiful daughter, the most beautiful who ever was; she was as white as snow and as red as blood, and once upon a time his daughter was stolen away, and he sent all his men to seek out his daughter, and he sent so many for so long, that he sent all his men out of his land."

"Who prepared his dinner, then?" Frolic asked.

"Either hear my tale, or kiss my tail," Madge said.

"Well said!" Fantastic said. "On with your tale, gammer."

Madge continued her tale:

"Oh, Lord, I quite forgot! There was a sorcerer, and this sorcerer could do anything, and he turned himself into a great dragon, and carried the king's daughter away in his mouth to a castle that he made of stone; and there he kept her I know not how long, until at last all the king's men went out so long that her two brothers went to seek her.

"Oh, I forget! She — I mean, he, the sorcerer — turned a handsome young man into a bear in the night, and into a man" — she meant an *old* man — "in the day, and he, the man, lived by a cross that marked a three-way intersection, and he, the sorcerer, made the enchanted handsome young man's sweetheart run mad."

She looked up and said, "By God's bones, who is coming here?"

CHAPTER 2

— Scene 2 —

Two brothers came to a cross that marked a three-way intersection.

"Be quiet, gammer," Frolic said. "Here some come to tell your tale for you."

"Let them alone," Fantastic said. "Let us hear what they will say."

"Upon these chalky cliffs of Albion — Great Britain's white cliffs of Dover — we are arrived now with tedious toil," the first brother said. "We are traveling the wide world round about, to seek our sister, fair Delia, wherever she is, yet we cannot so much as hear of her."

"Oh, cruel and unkind Lady Fortune!" the second brother said. "Unkind in that we cannot find our sister — our sister who is unfortunate in her very bad luck. But wait! Who have we here?"

He saw Erestus, an old man who was by the cross, stooping to gather plants for his food.

"Now, father, God be your speed!" the first brother said. "Good luck to you! What do you gather there?"

In this society, people called an old man "father" even when the old man was a stranger to them.

"Hips and haws, and sticks and straws, and things that I gather on the ground, my son," Erestus said.

Hips are rosehips, and haws are hawthorn berries. They are fruits.

"Hips and haws, and sticks and straws!" the first brother said. "Why, is that all your food, father?"

"Yes, son," Erestus replied.

"Father, here is an alms-penny for prayers for me," the second brother said, "and if I succeed in the project I am traveling for, I will give thee as good a gown of grey as ever thou did wear."

Religious pilgrims wore grey gowns.

"And, father, here is another alms-penny for me," the first brother said, "and if I succeed in my journey, I will give thee a palmer's staff of ivory, and a scallop shell of beaten gold."

A palmer is a religious pilgrim. Pilgrims who traveled to Jerusalem brought back a palm leaf, while pilgrims who traveled to the Shrine of St. James of Compostela in Galicia in northwest Spain brought back a scallop shell because it was a symbol of the saint.

Erestus, the old man, had the power of prophecy. He knew that they were seeking a woman.

"Was she fair?" Erestus asked. "Was she beautiful?"

"Yes, the fairest for white, and the purest for red, as the blood of the deer, or the driven snow," the second brother said.

"Then hark well, and mark well, my old spell," Erestus said.

In other words, listen carefully and pay attention to my old prophecy.

He continued:

"Be not afraid of every stranger.

"Don't shy away from every danger.

"Things that seem are not the same.

"Blow a blast of breath at every flame.

"For when one flame of fire goes out,

"Then come your wishes well about:

"If any ask who told you this good,
"Say, the White Bear of England's wood."
The first brother said, "Brother, did you hear what the old man said?

"Be not afraid of every stranger.
"Don't shy away from every danger.
"Things that seem are not the same.
"Blow a blast of breath at every flame.
"For when one flame of fire goes out,
"Then come your wishes well about:
"If any ask who told you this good,
"Say, the White Bear of England's wood."
The second brother said, "Well, if this should do us any good, then may the White Bear of England's wood fare well!"

The two brothers exited.

Talking to himself, Erestus said, "Now sit thee here, and tell a heavy, distressing tale, sad and serious in thy mood, and sober in thy cheer."

"Sober in thy cheer" meant 1) serious in your demeanor, and 2) frugal in your consumption of food. He was eating as he talked.

He continued, "Here sit thee now, and to thyself relate the hard misfortune of thy most wretched state. In Thessaly, land of witches and poisons, I lived in sweet happiness, until Lady Fortune worked my ruin, for there I was wedded to a dame who lived in honor, virtue, love, and fame. But Sacrapant, that cursed sorcerer, being besotted with my beauteous love, my dearest love, my true betrothed wife, sought the means to rid me of my life. But worse than this, he with his chanting and enchanting spells turned me immediately into an ugly bear, and when the sun settles in the west, then I begin to don my ugly hide, and all the day I sit, as now you see, and speak in hard-to-understand riddles, all inspired with prophetic 'rage' — inspiration. I seem to be an old and miserable man, and yet I am in the April of my age — I am actually a young man."

Venelia — his lady — appeared. Anyone observing her could tell she was insane.

"See where Venelia, my betrothed love, runs maddened and frenzied, all enraged, about the woods, all because of the sorcerer's cursed and enchanting spells," Erestus said.

Erestus had said he was "wedded" to Venelia, and he had called her "my true betrothed wife." Apparently, they were engaged to be married, which in this society was a legally binding contract, but the marriage ceremony had not yet occurred.

Venelia exited, and a man entered the scene.

Erestus said, "But here comes Lampriscus, my discontented neighbor."

Lampriscus, a beggar, was carrying a pot of honey.

"How are you now, neighbor?" Erestus said. "You look toward the ground as well as I. You are musing on —thinking about — something."

"Neighbor, I muse on nothing but on the matter I have so often talked to you about," Lampriscus said. "If you do anything for charity, help me. If you do anything for neighborhood or brotherhood, help me. Never was anyone so encumbered and burdened and troubled as is poor Lampriscus; and to begin, I ask you to please accept this pot of honey to improve your dietary fare."

"Thanks, neighbor, set it down; honey is always welcome to the Bear," Erestus said. "And now, neighbor, let me hear the cause of your coming."

"I am, as you know, neighbor, a man unmarried, and I lived so unquietly with my two wives that every year I keep holy both the days wherein I buried them," Lampriscus said. "My first wife was buried on Saint Andrew's day, the other on Saint Luke's."

Saint Andrew's day is November 30; Saint Luke's day is October 18.

Saint Andrew brought good luck to lovers.

October 18 was a day on which folklore said that young people could dream about their future spouse.

October 18 was also the day of the Horn Fair, leading to jokes about cuckolds: Men with unfaithful wives were said to grow invisible horns on their forehead.

"And now, neighbor, as you of this country — England — say, your custom is out — all the service you owed to your wives is paid," Erestus said. "But go on with your tale, neighbor."

"By my first wife, whose tongue wearied me when she was alive, and sounded in my ears like the clapper of a great bell, whose talk was a continual torment to all who dwelt by her or lived near her, you have heard me say I had an attractive daughter."

"True, neighbor," Erestus said.

"She it is who afflicts me with her continual clamors, and hangs on me like a burr," Lampriscus said. "Poor she is, and proud she is; she is as poor as a sheep newly shorn, and as proud of her hopes as a peacock is proud of her well-grown tail."

"Well said, Lampriscus!" Erestus said. "You speak it like an Englishman."

Lampriscus continued, "She is as quarrelsome and bad tempered as a wasp, and as stubborn and uncooperative as a child newly taken from the mother's teat; she is to my age as is smoke to the eyes, or as vinegar is to the teeth — she is very disagreeable."

Proverbs 10:26 states, "*As vinegar is to the teeth, and as smoke to the eyes, so* is *the slothful to them that send him*" (1599 Geneva Bible).

"Holily praised, neighbor," Erestus said, recognizing the allusion to the Bible. "Do as much for the next daughter."

"By my other wife, I had a daughter so hard-favored, so foul and ugly and ill-faced, that I think a grove full of golden trees, and the leaves of rubies and diamonds, would not be a dowry answerable to her deformity," Lampriscus said. "She is so ugly that even the dowry of a wealthy person would not get her married."

"Well, neighbor, now that you have spoken, hear me speak," Erestus said.

He prophesied:

"*Send them to the well for the water of life;*

"*There shall they find their fortunes unlooked for.*"

Revelation 21:6 states, "*And he said unto me, It is done, I am Alpha and Omega, the beginning and the end: I will give to him that is athirst, of the well of the water of life freely*" (1599 Geneva Bible).

Revelation 22:1 states, "*And he showed me a pure river of water of life, clear as crystal, proceeding out of the throne of God, and of the Lamb*" (1599 Geneva Bible).

Jesus speaks of the water of life to the Samaritan woman at Jacob's Well in John 4:10: "*Jesus answered and said unto her, If thou knewest that gift of God, and who it is that saith to thee, Give me drink, thou wouldest have asked of him, and he would have given thee water of life*" (1599 Geneva Bible).

In Christianity, the "water of life" is "living water" or "the Holy Spirit."

Erestus then said, "Neighbor, farewell."

"Farewell, and a thousand times farewell," Lampriscus said. "May you fare well indeed."

Erestus exited.

"And now goes poor Lampriscus to put in execution this excellent advice."

CHAPTER 3

— Scene 3 —

Frolic said, "Why, this goes round even without the musical accompaniment of a fiddling-stick."

"This goes round" means "This story is going well," but Frolic was punning on "round" as meaning a kind of song or dance. He also was saying that this story was as good an entertainment as a song or a dance.

He added, "But, listen, gammer, was this old man the man who was a bear in the night and a man in the day?"

"Yes, this is he!" Madge said. "And this man — Lampriscus — who came to him was a beggar, and dwelt upon a green.

"But be quiet! Who is coming here?

"Oh, these are the harvestmen — the reapers. Ten to one they sing a song of mowing — a song about cutting the grain with a scythe during harvest."

She would have lost her bet; the harvestmen sang a song of sowing, not mowing.

The harvestmen sang this song:

"All ye that lovely lovers be,

"Pray you for me.

"Lo, here we come a-sowing, a-sowing,

"And sow sweet fruits of love;

"In your sweet hearts well may it prove!"

Pleased with their song, they sang it again:

"All ye that lovely lovers be,

"Pray you for me.

"Lo, here we come a-sowing, a-sowing,

"*And sow sweet fruits of love;*
"*In your sweet hearts well may it prove!*"
The harvestmen exited.

CHAPTER 4

Huanebango and Booby the Clown arrived at the cross marking the crossroads. Huanebango was a braggart knight who carried a two-hand sword: It was long and heavy and required two hands to wield it, and it was old-fashioned.

"Gammer, who is he?" Fantastic asked.

"Oh, this is one who is going to the conjurer," Madge said. "Let him alone. Hear what he says."

Huanebango said, "Now, by Mars and Mercury, Jupiter and Janus, Sol and Saturn, Venus and Vesta, Pallas and Proserpina, and by the honor of my house — that is, my family, which is named Polimackeroeplacydus — it is a wonder to see what this love will make silly fellows risk, even in the wane of their wits and the infancy of their discretion — the decline of their intelligence and the immaturity of their judgment."

Mars is the god of war, and Mercury is the messenger god.

Jupiter is the King of the gods, and Janus is the two-faced god of doorways.

Sol is the Sun-god, and Saturn is the father of Jupiter and other Olympian gods.

Venus is the goddess of beauty, and Vesta is the goddess of the hearth.

Pallas is Minerva, aka Pallas Athena, the goddess of wisdom, and Proserpina is the goddess of vegetation.

Speaking to himself, and calling himself "friend," Huanebango continued, "Alas, my friend! What fortune calls thee forth to seek thy fortune among brass gates, enchanted towers, fire and brimstone, thunder and lightning? Beauty, I tell thee, is peerless and without equal, and she whom thou loves is precious. Do off and doff and do away with these desires, good countryman. Good friend, run away from thyself; and, as soon as thou can, forget her — that woman whom none must inherit but he who can tame monsters, achieve great deeds, solve riddles, loose and release people from enchantments, murder magic, and kill conjuring — and that is the great and mighty Huanebango!"

"Listen, sir, listen," Booby the Clown said. "First know I have here in my hat the flurting — flaunting — feather, and I have given the parish the start for the long stock."

He had run away from the parish where he had probably been an apprentice in order to follow Huanebango, who carried a long stock — a long sword.

Booby continued, "Now, sir, if it be no more but running through a little lightning and thunder, and 'riddle me, riddle me, what's this?' then I'll rescue the wench from the conjurer, even if he were ten conjurers."

"I have abandoned the court and honorable company, to do my devoir — duty — against this sore — troublesome — sorcerer and mighty magician," Huanebango said. "If this lady is as fair as she is said to be, she is mine, she is mine — *meus, mea, meum, in contemptum omnium grammaticorum*."

The Latin means "mine (masculine), mine (feminine), mine (neuter), in contempt of all grammar." Latin nouns have endings that indicate whether the noun is masculine, feminine, or neuter. *Femina* is Latin for woman; it is a feminine noun.

Booby said, "*O falsum Latinum!*"

The Latin means, "Oh, this is false — bad — Latin!"

He continued, "The fair maid is *minum, cum apurtinantibus gibletis* and all."

He was engaging in his own false Latin. By "minum," he may have meant "minus," which means "less" — he may have been calling the beautiful maiden a very small person. Or possibly, he meant "mine-um," meaning "mine." Giblets are guts. "*Cum apurtinantibus gibletis*" means "with her appertaining guts."

Huanebango said, "If she should be mine, as I assure myself the heavens will do something to reward my worthiness, she shall be allied to none of the meanest, least important gods, but be invested in the most famous stock and family of Huanebango Polimackeroeplacydus, my grandfather; my father, Pergopolineo; and my mother, Dionora de Sardinia, famously descended."

"Hear me, sir," Booby the Clown said. "Didn't you have a cousin who was called Gusteceridis?"

"Indeed, I had a cousin who sometimes followed the court unfortunately and without luck, and his name was Bustegusteceridis."

"Oh, lord, I know him well!" Booby the Clown said. "He is the knight of the neat's-feet."

A neat's-foot is the back of the heel of a cow or an ox. Bustegusteceridis is a notable knight of the table — he likes to eat.

"Oh, he loved no capon — a castrated cock (rooster) — better than a neat's-foot!" Huanebango said. "He has often cheated his boy-servant out of his dinner; that was his weakness, good Bustegusteceridis."

"Come, shall we go along on our way?" Booby the Clown asked.

He saw Erestus and said, "Wait! Here is an old man at the cross. Let us ask him the way there — the way to the castle of the evil sorcerer."

He called, "Ho, you gaffer! Please tell me where the wise man — the conjurer — dwells."

A gaffer is an old man — a grandfather.

In this society, a "wise man" or a "wise woman" was someone with knowledge of the occult.

Huanebango requested, "Please tell us where that earthly goddess — the commander of my thoughts, and the fair mistress of my heart — keeps her abode."

"Fair enough, and far enough from thy fingering, son," Erestus said.

To "finger" something means to "seize" something. It can also mean a certain kind of sexual act.

"I will follow my fortune after my own fancy, and act according to my own discretion," Huanebango said.

"Yet give something to an old man before you go," Erestus requested.

"Father, I think a piece of this cake might serve your need," Huanebango said.

"Yes, it would, son," Erestus said.

"Huanebango gives no cakes for alms," Huanebango said, referring to himself in the third person. "Ask those who give gifts for poor beggars."

He then pretended to speak to Delia: "Fair lady, if thou were once enshrined in this bosom, I would buckler — defend and shield — thee!"

He then imitated the sound of a military trumpet: "Haratantara."

He exited.

Booby the Clown said to Erestus, "Father, do you see this man — Huanebango? You wouldn't think he'll run a mile or two for such a cake, or care for a pudding. I tell you, father, he has kept up such a begging of me for a piece of this cake! Whoo! He comes upon me with 'a superfantial substance, and the foison — plenty — of the earth,' that I don't know what he means."

What did Booby the Clown mean? Probably the meaning was nonsensical. "Superfantial" could be a mistake for "superstantial," a philosophical term that means "formally existent, but not physically existent." A substance is physically existent, and so a superstantial substance is a contradiction in terms.

Booby the Clown said, "If he came to me thus, and said, 'my friend Booby,' or some such, why, I could spare him a piece with all my heart; but when he tells me how God has enriched me above other fellows with a cake, why, he makes me blind and deaf at once. Yet, father, here is a piece of cake for you, for the world is hard."

He gave Erestus some cake.

Erestus said, "Thanks, son, but listen to me:

"*He shall be deaf when thou shall not see.*

"Farewell, my son:

"*Things may so hit,*

"*Thou may have wealth to mend thy wit.*"

In other words:

"*Things may so happen that*

"*Thou may have wealth to make up for your lack of* intelligence."

"Farewell, father, farewell," Booby the Clown said, "for I must make haste after my two-hand sword — Huanebango — who has gone ahead."

He exited.

CHAPTER 5

— Scene 5 —

Sacrapant the Conjuror, alone in a room in his castle, said to himself, "The day is clear, the sky bright and gray. The lark is merry and sings her notes. Each thing rejoices underneath the sky, except for me, whom Heaven has in hate, wretched and miserable Sacrapant.

"In Thessaly I was born and brought up. My mother was named Meroe, she was a famous witch, and by her cunning knowledge I from her did learn to change and alter shapes of mortal men. There in Thessaly I turned myself into a dragon and stole away and kidnapped the daughter to the king, fair Delia, the mistress of my heart — the woman I love — and I brought her here to revive the man — me who seems in appearance to be young and pleasant to behold and yet in reality is aged, crooked, weak, and numb. Thus by enchanting spells I deceive those who behold and look upon my face. But I may as well bid youthful years adieu because she does not reciprocate my love.

"See where the woman comes from whom my sorrows grow!"

Delia, carrying a pot in her hand, entered the room.

"How are you now, fair Delia?" Sacrapant the Conjuror asked. "Where have you been?"

"At the foot of the rock for running water, and gathering roots for your dinner, sir," Delia said.

"Ah, Delia, thou are more beautiful than the running water. Yet thou are far harder than steel or adamant!"

Adamant is a legendary mineral noted for its hardness.

"Will it please you to sit down, sir?" Delia asked.

"Yes, Delia," Sacrapant the Conjuror said. "Sit and ask me for whatever thou want. Thou shall have it brought into thy lap."

"Then, I ask you, sir, please let me have the best food from the King of England's table, and the best wine in all France, brought in by the greatest scoundrel in all of Spain," Delia said.

"Delia, I am glad to see that you are so pleasant and joking," Sacrapant the Conjuror said. "Well, sit thee down."

He cast this spell:

"Spread, table, spread;

"Meat, drink, and bread,

"Ever [Always] may I have

"What I ever crave,

["Whatever I crave,]

"When I am spread:

"With meat for my black cock,

"And meat for my red."

Witches often had black cocks (roosters) and black cats as their familiar attending spirits.

The blood of a red cock (rooster) was sometimes used for medicinal purposes.

A friar entered with a joint of beef and a pot of wine.

"Here, Delia, will you fall to and eat?" Sacrapant the Conjuror asked.

"Is this the best meat in England?"

"Yes."

"What is it?"

"A joint of English beef, meat for a king and a king's followers."

"Is this the best wine in France?"

"Yes."

"What wine is it?"

"A cup of neat — undiluted — wine of Orleans, which has never come near the brewers in England," Sacrapant the Conjuror said.

Brewers in England diluted wine before they sold it.

"Is this the greatest knave in all Spain?" Delia asked.

"Yes."

"What is he? A friar?"

"Yes, a friar indefinite — of no particular order — and a knave infinite," Sacrapant the Conjuror said.

Delia said, "Then, I ask you, Sir Friar, tell me before you go: Who is the very greediest Englishman?"

"The miserable and most covetous usurious moneylender," the friar answered.

In this society, moneylenders were Jews.

"Hold thee there, friar," Sacrapant the Conjuror said. "Keep that opinion."

The friar exited.

"But, quiet! Who have we here? Who is coming?" Sacrapant the Conjuror said. "Delia, away, be gone!"

Delia's two brothers entered the grounds of the castle. Sacrapant saw them through a window, and they saw Delia.

Sacrapant the Conjuror said, "Delia, leave! For we are beset by two men."

He said to himself, "But Heaven — or Hell — shall rescue her for me."

Delia and Sacrapant the Conjuror exited.

"Brother, wasn't that Delia who did appear, or was it only her shadow — her ghost — that was here?" the first brother asked.

"Sister, where are thou?" the second brother called. "Delia, come again! He — that is, me — calls, who grieves because of thy absence."

He then said to Calypha, his brother, "Call out, Calypha, so that she may hear and cry aloud, for Delia is near."

An echo repeated the last word: "Near."

"Near!" the first brother said, "Oh, where? Have thou any news — any tidings?"

An echo repeated the last word: "Tidings."

"Which way is Delia, then?" the second brother asked. "Is it that way, or this?"

An echo repeated the last word: "This."

"And may we safely come where Delia is?" the first brother asked.

The echo did not repeat the last word but said, "Yes."

The "echo" was not an echo: The echo was the sorcerer Sacrapant, who was laying a trap for the two brothers.

The second brother asked the first brother, "Brother, do you remember the White Bear of England's wood? He prophesied:

"*Start not aside for every danger.*

"*Be not afraid of every stranger.*

"*Things that seem are not the same.*"

The first brother replied, "Brother, why don't we, then, courageously enter?"

"Then, brother, draw thy sword and follow me," the second brother said.

Sacrapant the Conjurer revealed himself. Lightning flashed and thunder sounded. The second brother fell down.

"What, brother, do thou fall?" the first brother asked.

"Yes, and thou, too, Calypha," Sacrapant the Conjurer said.

As a Thessalian sorcerer, he knew the brothers' names.

The first brother fell down.

Sacrapant the Conjurer ordered, "*Adestes, daemones*!"

The Latin means, "Come, demons!"

Two Furies — avenging spirits — arrived from out of Hell.

Sacrapant the Conjurer ordered, "Away with them! Go carry them straight to Sacrapant's cell, there in despair and torture to dwell."

A cell is a room or an apartment.

The two Furies exited with the two brothers.

The two brothers had followed the White Bear's prophecy. So far, the results seemed bad, but more events would follow.

Sacrapant the Conjurer said, "These are the sons of Thenores from Thessaly; they have come to seek Delia, their sister."

He had been born and raised in Thessaly, had fallen in love with Delia, who was the sister of the two brothers, and so had recognized the two brothers.

He continued, "But, with a potion I have given to her, my magic arts have made her forget who she is."

Sacrapant the Conjurer removed a section of turf and showed a light enclosed in a glass container.

He said, "See here the thing that prolongs my life. With this enchantment I can do anything. And until this light fades and dies, my magical skill shall always endure."

He prophesied:

"*And never shall anyone break this little glass.*

"*Except she who's neither wife, nor widow, nor maid.*

"*So then cheer thyself; this is thy destiny:*

"*Never to die — but by a dead man's hand.*"

CHAPTER 6

— Scene 6 —

Eumenides, a knight errant, aka wandering knight, arrived at the cross.

He said to himself, "Tell me, Time. Tell me, just Time:

"When shall I see Delia?

"When shall I see the loadstar — the guiding star — of my life?

"When shall my wandering course end with her sight,

"Or I but view my hope, my heart's delight?"

Seeing Erestus at the cross, he said, "Father, Godspeed! My best wishes to you! If you tell fortunes, please, good father, tell me mine."

Erestus gave the wandering knight advice and prophecies:

"Son, I do see in thy face

"Thy blessed fortune is coming apace.

"I do perceive that thou have intelligence and wit.

"Ask thy fate to govern it,

"For wisdom governed by good thinking and good advice,

"Makes many fortunate and wise.

"Bestow thy alms, give more than all —"

Erestus wanted Eumenides to give alms to the poor — and to give more than all.

Erestus continued his prophecy:

"Till dead men's bones come at thy call.

"Farewell, my son: dream of no rest,

"Till thou repent that which thou did best."

Erestus exited.

Eumenides said, "This man has left me in a labyrinth of perplexity:

"He tells me to *give more than all,*

"*Till dead men's bones come at my call;*

"He tells me to *dream of no rest,*

"*Till I repent that which I do best.*"

Despite the admonition to "dream of no rest," he immediately lay down and slept.

Wiggen, Corebus, the churchwarden, and the sexton arrived. Wiggen's and Corebus' friend Jack had died, and they wanted him buried quickly. The churchwarden and the sexton wanted money to pay for the burial.

"You may be ashamed, you whoreson, vile, contemptible scabby sexton and churchwarden, if you had any shame in those shameless faces of yours, to let a poor man lie so long above ground unburied," Wiggen said. "A rot on you all, you who have no more compassion for a good fellow when he is gone!"

"Would you have us bury him, and pay the costs ourselves to the parish treasury?" the churchwarden asked.

"Parish me no parishes," the sexton said. "Pay me my fees, and let the rest run on in the quarter's financial accounts, and put it down for one of your church's good deeds, in God's name! For I am not one who fastidiously stands upon the merits of the case."

The sexton wanted to make sure he got the money that was due to him, and he was OK with the parish bearing the rest of the cost of the funeral.

"You whoreson, sodden-headed sheep's face," Corebus said. "Shall a good fellow do less service and more honor to the parish, and yet you won't, when he is dead, let him have Christmas burial?"

Corebus sometimes made malapropisms. Instead of "less service," he meant "more service." Instead of "Christmas burial," he meant "Christian burial."

He, however, was gifted at invective. A person with a sodden head is one whose head is soaked with water — or alcohol. He was also saying that the sexton's head resembled that of a stupid sheep.

"Peace, Corebus! Quiet!" Wiggen said. "As sure as Jack was Jack, the most frolicsome franion — the merriest fellow — among you, and as sure as I, Wiggen, was his sweet sworn brother, Jack shall have his funeral rites, or some of them shall lie on God's dear earth for it, that's settled once and for all — that's for sure."

"Wiggen, I hope thou will do no more than thou dare to be held accountable for," the churchwarden said.

"Sir, sir, dare or dare not, more or less, answer or not answer, do this, or have this," Wiggen said.

Wiggen hit the churchwarden with a pike-staff. A pike-staff is a walking stick with a metal tip on one end.

The sexton cried, "Help, help, help! Wiggen sets upon the parish with a pike-staff."

The "parish" was the churchwarden, who was a parish official and the representative of the parish.

Eumenides the wandering knight woke up and came over to them.

"Hold thy hands, good fellow," he said to Wiggen. "Stop fighting."

Corebus said, "Can you blame him, sir, for taking Jack's side against this shake-rotten and corrupt parish who will not bury Jack?"

"Why, who was that Jack?" Eumenides asked.

"Who was Jack, sir?" Corebus said. "Who, our Jack, sir? Why, he was as good a fellow as ever trod upon neat's-leather."

Neat's leather is shoe leather. A neat is a cow or ox.

"Look, sir," Wiggen said to Eumenides. "He gave fourscore and nineteen — ninety-nine — mourning gowns to the parish when he died, and because he would not make the number of gowns a full hundred, they would not bury him."

According to Wiggen, Jack had given the church ninety-nine mourning gowns for the impoverished to wear at his funeral. This kind of thing is done for an aristocrat's funeral.

Wiggen asked sarcastically, "Isn't this good dealing?"

If Wiggen was correct about the gift, the good dealing was on Jack's part, not on the church's.

"Oh, Lord, sir, how he lies!" the churchwarden said. "Jack was not worth a halfpenny, and he drunk every penny, and now his fellows, his drunken companions, would have us bury him at the expense of the parish. If we make many such 'bargains,' we may as well pull down the steeple, sell the roof and bells, and use cheap thatch as the roof for the chancel. Jack shall lie above ground until he dances a lively galliard about the churchyard, as far as I, Steven Loach, am concerned."

The chancel is the part of the church near the altar.

"*Sic argumentaris, Domine* Loach," Wiggen said.

The Latin means, "Thus you argue, Master Loach."

Wiggen added, "You say, 'If we make many such 'bargains,' we may as well pull down the steeple, sell the bells, and use cheap thatch as the roof for the chancel — in good time, sir, and hang yourself in the bell ropes, when you have done. *Domine, opponens praepono tibi hanc quaestionem —*"

The Latin means, "Master, in opposition, I put before you this question."

He continued, "— will you have the ground broken to bury Jack or your heads broken first? For one of them shall be done at once, and to begin acting my preference, I'll seal it upon your coxcomb."

He meant that he would begin beating their heads.

Jesters, aka Fools, wore hats that resembled the coxcomb of a cock.

"Hold thy hands, please, good fellow," Eumenides said. "Don't be too hasty."

Corebus said, "You capon's face — you who have the face of a castrated cock — we shall have you turned out of the parish one of these days, with not even a tatter of clothing to cover your arse; then you will be in a worse condition than Jack."

Perhaps he was talking to the churchwarden.

"Indeed, and his condition is bad enough," Eumenides said.

He then said to the churchwarden, "This fellow is just doing the part of a friend: He seeks to bury his friend. How much money will it take to bury him?"

"Indeed, about some fifteen or sixteen shillings will bury him respectably," Wiggen said.

"Aye, or even thereabouts, sir," the sexton said. "Therabouts" could have referred to the "fifteen or sixteen shillings" or to the adjective "respectably."

"Here, take it, then," Eumenides said.

As he counted out the money, he said to himself, "And I have left for me only one poor three half-pence. Now I remember the words the old man spoke at the cross:

"'*Bestow all thou have'* — and this is all —

"'*till dead men's bones come at thy call.*'"

Eumenides then said, "Here, take it, and so farewell."

He gave the money to the churchwarden.

Wiggen said, "May God, and all good, be with you, sir!"

Eumenides exited.

Wiggen then said to the churchwarden and the sexton, "You cormorants, I'll bestow one peal of the church bell for Jack at my own proper costs and charges."

Cormorants are greedy seabirds.

Corebus said to the churchwarden and the sexton, "You may thank God the long staff and the bilbo-blade didn't cross your coxcomb. You're lucky we didn't beat you."

A bilbo-blade is a sword, so called because good swords were made in Bilboa, Spain.

He then said to Wiggen, "Well, we'll go to the church-stile and have a pot of ale."

He imitated the sound of drinking: "Trill-lill."

Often, an alehouse was located at the stile at the entrance of a churchyard. A stile allowed people but not herding animals to cross a fence. Alehouses and churches were the main places of social interaction in villages.

Corebus and Wiggen exited.

The churchwarden said to the sexton, "Come, let's go."

They exited in a different direction from that of Corebus and Wiggen.

CHAPTER 7

Fantastic said, "But listen, gammer, I think that this Jack had a great influence in the parish."

"Oh, this Jack was a marvelous fellow!" Madge said. "He was just a poor man, but very well beloved. You shall see soon what this Jack will come to."

The harvestmen arrived, holding hands with the harvestwomen.

"Quiet!" Frolic said. "Who do we have here? Our amorous harvesters."

"Aye, aye, let us sit still, and let them alone," Fantastic said.

The harvestmen sang this song:

"Lo, here we come a-reaping, a-reaping,

"To reap our harvest-fruit!

"And thus we pass the year so long,

"And never be we mute."

Pleased with their song, they sang it again:

"Lo, here we come a-reaping, a-reaping,

"To reap our harvest-fruit!

"And thus we pass the year so long,

"And never be we mute."

CHAPTER 8

Huanebango stood outside Sacrapant's Castle.

"Quiet!" Frolic said. "Who have we here?"

"Oh, this is an ill-tempered gentleman!" Madge said. "All you who love your lives, keep out of the smell — the range — of his two-hand sword. Now he goes to see the conjurer."

"I think the conjurer should put the fool into a conjuring-box," Fantastic said.

Some kinds of conjuring-boxes are used to make people disappear.

Huanebango recited these lines:

"Fee, fa, fum, here is the Englishman,

'Conquer him who can,

"Come for his lady bright.

"To prove himself a knight,

"And win her love in fight."

Booby the Clown arrived. Not seeing Huanebango, he said, "Who-haw, Master Bango, are you here?"

Seeing Huanebango, Booby said, "Listen, you had best sit down here, and beg for an alms with me."

The alms would be entrance into the castle.

Huanebango replied, "Hence, base cullion!"

Literally, a "cullion" is a testicle. Figuratively, it is a rascal.

He continued, "Here is a man — me — who commands his ingress and egress — his entering and exiting — with his weapon, and will enter at his own voluntary wish and free will, no matter whosoever says no."

A voice said, "No."

A flame of fire shot upward, and Huanebango fell down, clanging his sword on a rock.

"So with that they — Huanebango and the ground — kissed, and spoiled the edge of as good a two-hand sword as ever God put life in," Madge said. "Now goes Booby in, in spite of the conjurer."

Sacrapant, whose voice had said, "No," and two Furies entered the scene.

"Take him away into the open fields, to be a ravening prey to crows and kites," Sacrapant said.

Actually, the crows and kites — birds of prey — were ravening: They were ravenous. Sacrapant may have deliberately used the oxymoron to describe a moron.

The two Furies carried out Huanebango.

Sacrapant added, "And as for this villain, let him wander up and down in nothing but darkness and eternal night."

He struck Booby blind.

Using a nickname for Huanebango, Booby the Clown said, "Here have thou slain Huan, a slashing, spirited knight, and robbed poor Booby of his sight."

A slashing knight is a swashbuckler, which literally means a person who noisily hits another person's buckler, aka shield.

"Go away from here, villain, go away!" Sacrapant ordered.

Booby exited.

"Now I have given a potion of forgetfulness to Delia," Sacrapant said, "so that, when she comes, she shall not know her brothers. Look, where they labor, like rural slaves; with spade and mattock, they dig and loosen this enchanted ground!"

A mattock is a kind of pickaxe.

He continued, "Now I will call her by another name, for *never shall she know herself again until Sacrapant has breathed his last.*"

He looked up and said, "See where she comes."

Delia entered the scene.

"Come here, Delia, take this goad for prodding cattle," Sacrapant said. "Here hard at hand two slaves work and dig for gold. Gore — wound — them with this, and thou shall have enough."

He handed her a goad.

"Good sir, I don't know what you mean," Delia said.

"She has forgotten to be Delia, but she has not forgotten as much as she should forget," Sacrapant said to himself.

She was talking to him using formal words such as "sir" and "you." Sacrapant wanted her to like him and use the informal, familiar words "thou" and "thee" when talking to him.

Sacrapant said to himself, "But I will change her name."

He then said to Delia, using her new name, "Fair Berecynthia, for so this country calls you, go spur these strangers, wench; they dig for gold."

The goddess Cybele, protector of castles, was worshipped on a mountain named Berecynthia.

Sacrapant exited.

"Oh, heavens, how I am beholden to this handsome young man!" Delia said about Sacrapant.

Because of his sorcery, he appeared to her to be a handsome young man.

She then said, "But I must spur these strangers to do their work. See where they come."

Her two brothers, in their undershirts, were digging with spades.

"Oh, brother, see where Delia is!" the first brother said.

"Oh, Delia, we are happy to see thee here!" the second brother said.

"Why are you telling me about Delia, you prating, chattering country workers?" Delia said. "I know no Delia, nor do I know what you mean. Apply yourselves to your work, or else you're likely to smart when I prod you with my goad."

"Why, Delia, don't thou know thy brothers here?" the first brother asked. "We have come from Thessaly to seek thee, and thou deceive thyself, for thou are Delia."

"Yet more of Delia?" she said. "Then take this, and smart."

She pricked them with the goad and then said, "Do you devise tricks to defer your labor? Work, villains, work; it is for gold you dig."

"Be quiet, brother, be calm," the second brother said. "This vile enchanter has completely stolen away Delia's senses, and she forgets that she is Delia."

"Cease, cruel thou, thou who hurt the miserable," the first brother said to Delia.

He then said to the second brother, "Dig, brother, dig, for she is hard as steel. "

They dug, and they saw a light in a glass under a little hill.

"Stop, brother," the second brother said. "What have thou revealed?"

"Go away, and don't touch it," Delia said. "It is something that my lord has hidden there."

After she covered it again, Sacrapant returned.

"Well done!" he said to her. "Thou drive these diggers well."

He then ordered the two brothers, "Go get you inside, you laboring slaves."

The two brothers exited.

Sacrapant said to Delia, "Come, Berecynthia, let us go inside likewise, and hear the nightingale sing her notes."

CHAPTER 9

Zantippa, the ill-tempered daughter, walked to the Well of Life with a pitcher in her hand.

"Now for a husband, house, and home," she said to herself, "May God send me a good husband or none, I pray to God! My father has sent me to the well for the water of life, and he tells me that if I speak fair, flattering words, I shall have a husband. But here comes Celanta, my sweet sister. I'll stand nearby and hear what she says."

Celanta, the ugly wench, walked to the well for water with a pitcher in her hand.

"My father has sent me to the well for water, and he tells me that if I speak fair, flattering words, I shall have a husband, and none of the worst," she said to herself. "Well, though I am black, I am sure all the world will not forsake me; and, as the old proverb is, though I am black, I am not the devil."

The word "black" meant "with a dark complexion." In this society, the devil was said to be black. This culture valued light complexions; it regarded dark complexions as ugly.

Zantippa came forward and said, "Marry-gup with a murren."

This was an oath meaning "A pox on you!"

She continued, "I know why thou spoke that, but go thy ways home as wise as thou came, or I'll send thee home with a wanion — a vengeance."

She struck her pitcher against her sister's pitcher, broke them both, and then exited.

"I think that she is the curstest quean — most ill-tempered hussy — in the world," Celanta said. "You see what she is, a little pretty, but as proud as the devil, and the veriest vixen — the greatest shrew — who lives upon God's earth. Well, I'll let her alone, and go home, and get another pitcher, and, for all this, get myself to the well again for water."

She exited.

The two Furies carried Huanebango out of Sacrapant's living chamber and lay him by the Well of Life, and then they exited.

Carrying a pitcher, Zantippa, the pretty but ill-tempered daughter, returned to the well.

She said to herself, "Once again I am here for a husband; and, indeed, Celanta, I have got the head start on you; perhaps husbands grow by the well-side.

"Now my father says I must control my tongue. Why, alas, what am I, then? A woman without a tongue is like a soldier without his weapon, but I'll have my water, and then be gone."

A proverb stated, "A woman's weapon is her tongue."

Zantippa dipped her pitcher in the well.

A Voice came out of the well and said this:

"*Gently dip, but not too deep,*

"*For fear you make the golden beard to weep.*

A Head came up out of the Well of Life with ears of corn dangling from its hair and said this:

"*Fair maiden, white and red,*

"*Comb me smooth, and stroke my head,*

"*And thou shall have some cockell-bread.*"

Cockell-bread was the name of a bawdy game played by maidens in which they pretended to knead bread dough with their buttocks while singing a song. According to folklore, if a maiden kneaded the dough in this way, baked the bread, and gave it to a young man to eat, it would act as a love charm. The Head meant that Zantippa would find a husband.

Such bawdiness may be appropriate. Zantippa had gone to the Well of Life for a husband and the water of life, and the impregnating fluid of life is semen.

Zantippa said, "What is this?

"Fair maiden, white and red,

"Comb me smooth, and stroke my head,

"And thou shall have some cockell-bread"?

"'Cockell,' do thou call it, boy? Indeed, I'll give you cockell-bread."

Angered by the bawdiness implicit in "cockell-bread," she broke her pitcher upon the Head. Thunder sounded and lightning flashed.

Huanebango, whom Sacrapant had made deaf, rose.

He said, "Philida, phileridos, pamphilida, florida, flortos."

This is nonsense that sounds like Spanish.

He then said, "Dub dub-a-dub, bounce, said the guns, with a sulphurous huff-snuff."

"Dub dub-a-dub" is an imitation of drumming. "Bounce" means "bang." "A sulphurous huff-snuff" is the smell coming from a fired gun or cannon.

He then said, "Waked by a wench, pretty peat, pretty love, and my sweet pretty pigsnie."

"Pretty peat" means "pretty girl." "Pigsnie" literally means "pig's eye," but it figuratively means "sweetheart."

He then said, "Just by thy side shall sit me, who is surnamed great Huanebango. Safe in my arms will I keep thee, no matter whether Mars threatens, or Olympus thunders."

He put his arms around her.

Zantippa said to herself, "Ugh, what greasy groom — greasy man — have we here? He looks as though he crept out of the backside of the well, and he speaks like a drum whose skin has split at the west end."

Huanebango said, "Oh, that I might — but I may not, woe to my destiny therefore! — kiss what I clasp! But I cannot. Tell me, my destiny, why?"

Apparently, Sacrapant's spell had made Huanebango both deaf and unable to kiss Zantippa.

Also, perhaps, Huanebango's destiny had changed. In his short speech, he mentioned "destiny" twice. His first "destiny" was to rescue Delia from Sacrapant the Conjuror, but now he believed his "destiny" was to marry Zantippa.

"Whoop!" Zantippa said to herself. "Now I have my dream — I have my husband. Did you ever hear so great a wonder as this: three blue beans in a blue bladder — rattle, bladder, rattle?"

To her, Huanebango's babbling was like the sound of beans in a baby's rattle.

Huanebango said to himself, "I'll now set my countenance, and speak to her in prose. It may be that this rim-ram-ruff is too rude an encounter."

His babbling — his rim-ram-ruff — had been an attempt at poetic flirting, an attempt that had failed.

He said, "Let me, fair lady, if you are at leisure, revel with your sweetness, and rant about that cowardly conjurer who has cast me, or congealed — frozen — me rather, into an unkind sleep, and polluted my carcass — he has violated my body."

"Laugh, laugh, Zantippa," she said to herself. "Thou have thy fortune: a fool and a husband under one."

She intended to be the boss of the two.

"Truly, sweetheart, I am as I seem to be, about some twenty years old, in the very April of my age," Huanebango said.

"Why, what a chattering ass is this!" Zantippa said to herself.

Huanebango began to speak love poetry:

"Her coral lips, her crimson chin,

"Her silver teeth so white within,

"Her golden locks, her rolling eye,

"Her pretty parts, let them without comment go by,

"Heigh-ho, have wounded me,

"That I must die this day to see!"

The "pretty parts" may be those underneath clothing. "Heigh-ho" is a sigh. In this culture, "to die" meant "to have an orgasm."

"By Gogs-bones, thou are a flouting, mocking knave," Zantippa said. "'Her coral lips, her crimson chin!' he says, wilshaw!"

"By Gogs-bones" is an oath meaning "By God's bones."

Zantippa was playing with words. "Wil" comes from a now obsolete Welsh word meaning "tricky." (Think of "wily.") Huanebango's flouting, mocking words (he would call them poetic words) were tricky. She was saying "wil-shaw" rather than "p-shaw." "Wil-shaw" combines the meanings of "tricky" and "pshaw."

"True, my own, and my own because mine, and mine because mine, ha, ha!" Huanebango said. "Above a thousand pounds in possibility, and things fitting thy desire in possession."

Huanebango was detailing his income: His lands provided him up to a thousand pounds annually.

Zantippa said to herself, "The sot thinks I ask about his lands. Lob be your comfort, and cuckold be your destiny!"

"Lob" means "clown" or "lout." "Lob's pound" is a slang term for "prison," and Huanebango's new "comfort" as a hen-pecked husband could be similar to being in prison.

His new destiny is to be a cuckold: a man with an unfaithful wife.

Zantippa said to him, "Listen, sir; if you will have us, you had best say so in good time — you had best propose to me right away."

In referring to herself as "us," she was using the majestic plural.

"True, sweetheart, and I will royalize thy progeny — children — with my pedigree," he replied.

This may be a happy marriage. Huanebango, being deaf, will not know that Zantippa is a shrew. His deafness will also help her hide her unfaithfulness. Huanebango takes pride in his ancestry, and Zantippa is a proud woman. Being married to a person with important ancestors is something to brag about.

Earlier, Erestus had prophesied to Booby the Clown, "*He shall be deaf when thou shall not see.*"

The prophecy had come true.

Booby the Clown, while Huanebango was blind.

CHAPTER 10

Eumenides stood on a nearby road.

He said to himself, "Wretched Eumenides, still unfortunate, hated by fortune and forlorn by fate, here waste away and die, wretched Eumenides. Die in the spring, the April of my age! Here sit thee down, repent what thou have done: I wish to God that it were never begun!"

He was repenting that which he had done best: resolve to rescue the princess from the evil sorcerer. Earlier, Erestus had told him this:

"Farewell, my son: dream of no rest,

"Till thou repent that which thou did best."

The Ghost of Jack came up from behind him and said, "You are well overtaken, sir."

A polite traveler would customarily say that to another traveler he had caught up to.

"Who's that?" Eumenides asked.

"You are heartily well met, sir," the Ghost of Jack, invisible, said, giving him a playful pinch.

"Stop it, I say," Eumenides said. "Who is that who pinches me?"

In this culture, ghosts often pinched people, sometimes maliciously.

The Ghost of Jack now materialized behind Eumenides and then stood where Eumenides could see him.

The Ghost of Jack said, "Trusting in God, good Master Eumenides, that you are in so good health as all your friends were at the making hereof, may God give you a good morning, sir!"

The Ghost of Jack was assuming that Eumenides' friends had toasted his health, and God had responded by actually making Eumenides healthy. In this culture, some letters began with this kind of salutation. Travellers also often greeted each other by wishing that God would give the other a good morning. The Ghost of Jack was being very respectful to Eumenides.

The Ghost of Jack then asked, "Don't you need a neat, competent, handsome, and clean young lad, about the age of fifteen or sixteen years, who can run by your horse, and, when needed, make your mastership's shoes as black as ink?"

Footmen literally ran by their master's horse.

The Ghost of Jack then asked, "How do you answer me, sir?"

Eumenides, who apparently did not know that this was a ghost, said, "Alas, pretty lad, I don't know how I will provide for myself, much less a servant, my pretty boy, because my state of finances is so bad."

"Be content," the Ghost of Jack said, "You shall not be so ill a master but I'll be as bad a servant. Tut, sir, I know you, though you don't know me. Aren't you the man, sir — deny it if you can, sir — who came from a strange place in the land of Catita, where a jackanapes flies with his tail in his mouth. Didn't you come here to seek out a lady as white as snow and as red as blood?"

The Ghost of Jack continued to be playful. Catita is a fairy-tale land with fairytale creatures such as a jackanapes (which is usually a monkey), but it is true that Eumenides came from a faraway land — perhaps even Catita — and that he came here to seek and find a lady.

"Ha, ha!" the Ghost of Jack said. "Have I now said something that touches you closely?"

"I think this boy is a spirit," Eumenides said to himself, beginning to catch on to the truth. "Someone who knows such private matters must be a ghost."

He then asked, "How do thou know all this?"

The Ghost of Jack said, "Tut, aren't you the man, sir — deny it if you can, sir — who gave all the money you had to the burying of a poor man, and had only one three-half-pence coin left in your purse? Be satisfied, sir, that I'll serve you, that is certain."

"Well, my lad, since thou are so insistent, I am happy to entertain — employ — thee, not as a servant, but as a copartner in my journey," Eumenides said. "But to where shall we go? For I have not any money more than one bare three-half-pence coin."

"Well, master, be content," the Ghost of Jack said, "for unless my divination is wrong, that shall be spent at the next inn or alehouse we come to; for, master, I know you are exceedingly hungry. Therefore, I'll go ahead of you and provide dinner for when you come; no doubt but you'll come fair and softly — that is, at your own leisure — after me."

"Aye, go before me; I'll follow thee."

"But listen, master? Do you know my name?"

"No, I promise thee, not yet."

"Why, I am Jack."

"Jack!" Eumenides said.

Realizing that he was talking to a ghost, he said, "Why, so be it, then."

CHAPTER 11

At an inn, the hostess and the Ghost of Jack set food on the table and fiddlers came to play. Eumenides walked up and down, and he would eat no food.

"What do you say, sir?" the hostess asked him. "Do you please to sit down?"

"Hostess, I thank you," Eumenides said. "I have no great appetite."

"Please, sir, what is the reason your master is so strange?" the hostess asked the Ghost of Jack. "Doesn't this food please him?"

"Yes, it does please him, hostess, but it is my master's custom to pay before he eats; therefore, give us the bill, good hostess."

"Indeed, you shall have it, sir, quickly," the hostess replied.

She exited.

"Why, Jack, what do thou mean?" Eumenides said. "Thou know I haven't any money; therefore, sweet Jack, tell me what shall I do?"

"Well, master, look in your purse," the Ghost of Jack replied.

"Why, indeed, it is foolish to do that, for I have no money."

"Why, look, master," the Ghost of Jack said. "Do that much for me."

"Looking into his purse, Eumenides said, "Alas, Jack, my purse is full of money!"

Why "alas"? Is it necessarily a good idea to take money from a ghost?

"You say 'alas,' master!" the Ghost of Jack said. "Is that word appropriate to this situation? Why, I think I should have seen you cast away your cloak, and in a bravado make a show of joy as you danced a lively galliard-dance round about the room. Why, master, your manservant can teach you more intelligence than this."

The hostess returned.

The Ghost of Jack said, "Come, hostess, cheer up my master."

"You are heartily welcome," the hostess said to Eumenides, "and may it please you to eat a fat capon — a fairer bird, a finer bird, a sweeter bird, a crisper bird, a more skillfully prepared bird — that your worship has never eaten the like of before."

"Thanks, my fine, eloquent hostess," Eumenides said.

"But listen, master, to one word by the way," the Ghost of Jack said. "Are you content that I shall get halves and share equally in all you get in your journey?"

"I am, Jack," Eumenides said. "Here is my hand."

They shook hands.

Eumenides now trusted the Ghost of Jack.

"Enough, master, I ask no more," the Ghost of Jack said.

"Come, hostess, receive your money, and I thank you for my good entertainment," Eumenides said.

He gave her money.

"You are heartily welcome, sir," she replied.

"Come, Jack, to where shall we go now?" Eumenides asked.

"Indeed, master, let's go to the conjurer's immediately."

"I am happy to do that, Jack," Eumenides said.

He then said, "Hostess, farewell."

Eumenides and the Ghost of Jack exited.

Oddly, Eumenides seems to have left without eating. He may have taken the food with him because he wanted to hurry to the conjurer's castle.

CHAPTER 12

Booby the Clown and Celanta, the ugly wench, went to the Well of Life for water.

Booby, who was blind, said, "Come, my duck, come. I have now got a wife. Thou are fair, aren't thou?"

Celanta, the ugly wench, said, "My Booby, I am the fairest and most beautiful wench alive; have no doubt about that."

"Come, wench, are we almost at the well?" Booby asked.

"Aye, Booby, we are almost at the well now," Celanta replied. "I'll go fetch some water. Sit down while I dip my pitcher in."

A Voice came out of the well and said this:

"*Gently dip, but not too deep,*

"*For fear you make the golden beard to weep.*

Celanta gently dipped her pitcher in the well.

A Head came up out of the Well of Life with ears of corn dangling from its hair and said this:

"*Fair maiden, white and red,*

"*Comb me smooth, and stroke my head,*

"*And thou shall have some cockell-bread.*"

Celanta combed — raked with her fingers — the ears of corn onto her lap. The corn silk resembled a golden beard.

Another Voice came out of the well and said this:

"*Gently dip, but not too deep,*

"*For fear thou make the golden beard to weep.*

Celanta gently dipped her pitcher in the well.

A Second Head came up out of the Well of Life with ingots of gold dangling from its hair and said this:

"Fair maiden, white and red,
"Comb me smooth, and stroke my head,
"And every hair a sheaf shall be,
"And every sheaf a golden tree."

Celanta combed — raked with her fingers — the gold onto her lap. The gold dangled from the Second Head and resembled a golden beard. By being kind to the First Head, Celanta had reaped a golden beard of corn. Because she had been kind to the First Head, she was given the chance to be kind to the Second Head and reap a golden beard of gold. Her kindness had made both Heads call her a "fair maiden."

"Oh, see, Booby, I have combed a great deal of gold onto my lap, and a great deal of corn!" Celanta said.

"Well done, wench!" Booby the Clown said. "Now we shall have toast enough. May God send us coiners — makers of coins — to coin our gold. But come, shall we go home, sweetheart?"

He wanted the ears of corn to be made into toasted cornbread, and the gold to be made into gold coins.

"Come, Booby, I will lead you."

Talking to himself, Booby said, "So, Booby, the prophecy has come true:

"Things have well hit;
"Thou have gotten wealth to mend thy wit."

"Well hit" means "ended well."

This may be a happy marriage. Booby, being blind, will think that Celanta is beautiful. Indeed, her kindness makes her beautiful.

CHAPTER 13

— Scene 13 —

The Ghost of Jack and Eumenides stood outside Sacrapant's Castle.

"Come away, master, come," the Ghost of Jack said.

"Go along, Jack, I'll follow thee," Eumenides replied. "Jack, they say it is good to go cross-legged and say one's prayers backwards. What do you think?"

Actually, saying prayers backwards is usually associated with black magic; however, some authorities say that reciting spells backwards can be used to reverse spells. Eumenides may have been misspeaking out of nervousness about meeting the sorcerer. Fortunately, the Ghost of Jack, as a spirit, knew what to do.

"Tut, never fear, master; leave it to me," the Ghost of Jack said. "Here sit you still; speak not a word, and so that you shall not be enticed with Sacrapant's enchanting speeches, I'll stop your ears with this wool I am holding."

In Homer's *Odyssey*, Odysseus stopped the ears of his men with wax so that they would not hear the enticing, enchanting songs of the Sirens. Odysseus heard the songs, but he had first taken the precaution of having his men tie him to the mast of the ship they were on so that he would not jump overboard and swim to the Sirens.

The Ghost of Jack put wool in Eumenides' ears and then said, "And so, master, sit still, for I must go to the conjurer."

He exited.

Sacrapant the Conjuror entered the scene, saw Eumenides, and said, "What is this! What man are thou, who sit so sad?

Why do thou gaze upon these stately trees without the permission and wish of Sacrapant?"

Following Jack the Ghost's orders, Eumenides did not speak to Sacrapant.

Sacrapant the Conjuror waited a moment and then said, "What, not a word, but mum? Then, Sacrapant, thou are betrayed."

He realized that someone had known to put wool in this person's ears. Someone of the spirit world must be acting against Sacrapant. He also realized his magic was failing because he did not know who this person was.

The Ghost of Jack returned, invisible to Sacrapant, and took Sacrapant's wreath from his head and his sword out of his hand.

Sacrapant the Conjuror said, "What hand invades the head of Sacrapant? What hateful Fury does maliciously envy my happy state? Then, Sacrapant, these are thy last moments alive. Alas, my veins are numbed, and my muscles shrink. My blood is pierced, my breath fleeting away. And now my timeless date — what I hoped would be my eternal life — has come to an end! He — me — in whose life has committed so foul deeds, now with his death his soul descends to Hell."

He died, and the two Furies entered the scene and dragged his body away.

"Oh, sir, have you gone?" the Ghost of Jack said. "Now I hope we shall have some other trouble."

More actions remained to be performed. People would have to take time and make an effort to perform them.

"Now, master, how do you like this?" the Ghost of Jack asked Eumenides. "The conjurer is dead, and he vows never to trouble us more. Now get you to your fair lady, and see what you can do with her."

Eumenides did not reply.

The Ghost of Jack said, "Alas, he did not hear me all this while! But I will help with that."

He pulled the wool out of Eumenides' ears.

"Hello, Jack," Eumenides said. "What news do you have?"

"Here, master, take this sword, and dig with it at the foot of this hill," the Ghost of Jack said.

Jack gave Eumenides the sword, Eumenides dug at the foot of the little hill, and he found a light in a glass.

"Hey, Jack! What is this?"

"Master, without this the conjurer could do nothing; and so long as this light lasts, so long does his magical art endure, and once this light is out, then his magical art decays."

"Why, then, Jack, I will soon put out this light."

"I see, master," the Ghost of Jack said. "How?"

"Why, with a stone I'll break the glass, and then blow it out."

"No, master, you may as soon break the blacksmith's anvil as this little vial," the Ghost of Jack said. "Nor can the biggest blast that ever Boreas, the north wind, blew blow out this little light; but she who is not maiden, nor wife, nor widow can blow it out with her breath. Master, blow this horn, and see what will happen."

He gave Eumenides the horn.

Eumenides blew the horn. Venelia, the betrothed of Erestus, entered, broke the glass, blew out the light, and then exited.

Sacrapant's prophecy had come true. Earlier, he had said this:

"*And never shall anyone break this little glass.*

"Except she who's neither wife, nor widow, nor maiden.
"So then cheer thyself; this is thy destiny:
"Never to die — but by a dead man's hand."

Erestus had called Venelia his betrothed wife, but he meant that they were engaged to be married. In this society, this was a legally binding agreement.

The marriage ceremony had not yet happened, so she was not yet a wife.

Of course, she was not a widow.

As to not being a maiden, this may mean 1) she was not an old maiden, and/or 2) she was not unattached and so was not a maiden, and/or 3) Erestus and she had had sex, something not uncommon after the betrothal.

"So, master, how do you like this?" the Ghost of Jack said. "This is the woman who ran mad in the woods, the betrothed love of the man who keeps the cross; and now, this light being out, all are restored to their former liberty and freedom from Sacrapant's spells, and now, master, go to the lady whom you have so long looked for."

The Ghost of Jack opened a door leading into the castle and then drew a curtain, revealing Delia sitting in a chair, asleep.

Eumenides recited a magic chant:

"God speed, fair maiden, sitting alone – there is once.

"God speed, fair maiden, sitting alone – there is twice.

"God speed, fair maiden, sitting alone – that is thrice."

Delia woke up during Eumenides' reciting of the spell and said, "I am not sitting alone, good sir, for you are nearby."

"That is enough, master, she has spoken," the Ghost of Jack said. "Now I will leave her with you."

Eumenides said to Delia, "Thou fairest flower of these western parts, whose beauty so reflects in my sight as does a crystal mirror in the sun, for thy sweet sake I have crossed the frozen Rhine. Leaving the fair Po, I sailed up the Danube, as far as the land of Saba; the Danube's rising waters cut between the Tartars and the Russians: These have I crossed for thee, fair Delia."

The Rhine, Po, and Danube are all rivers.

Eumenides then said, "So then grant me that which I have sought for so long."

"Thou gentle knight, whose fortune is so good to find me out and set my brothers free, my faith, my heart, my hand I give to thee," Delia said.

"Thanks, gentle madam," Eumenides said, "but here comes Jack; thank him, for he is the best friend whom we have."

The Ghost of Jack, carrying Sacrapant's head in his hand, entered the scene.

"Hello, Jack!" Eumenides said. "What have thou there?"

"Indeed, master, the head of the conjurer."

"Why, Jack, that is impossible," Eumenides said. "He was a young man."

Jack was carrying the head of an old man.

"Ah, master, he deceived all who beheld him!" the Ghost of Jack said. "But he was a miserable, old, and crooked man, though to each man's eye he seemed young and fresh, because, master, this conjurer took the shape of the 'old' man who kept the cross, and that 'old' man was in the likeness of the conjurer. But now, master, blow your horn."

Eumenides blew his horn.

Venelia (Erestus' betrothed), Delia's two brothers (who were named Thelea and Calypha), and the 'old' man who kept the cross (Erestus) entered the scene. Now that Sacrapant's spells had been broken, Erestus had resumed his real appearance as a young man and Venelia was no longer insane.

"Welcome, Erestus!" Eumenides said. "Welcome, fair Venelia! Welcome, Thelea and Calypha both! Now I have her whom I have sought so long — so says fair Delia, if we have your — her brothers' — consent."

The first brother said, "Valiant Eumenides, thou well deserve to have our favor, so let us rejoice that by thy means we are at liberty. Here may we rejoice in each other's sight, and may this fair lady have her wandering knight."

"So, master, now you think you have accomplished your mission, but I must say something to you," the Ghost of Jack said. "You know that you and I were partners, and I am to have half in all you have gotten."

"Why, so thou shall, Jack," Eumenides said.

"Why, then, master, draw your sword, divide your lady into two halves, and let me have half of her immediately," the Ghost of Jack said.

"Why, I hope, Jack, thou are only jesting," Eumenides said. "I promised thee half of what I got, but not half my lady."

"But what else, master?" the Ghost of Jack said. "Have you not gotten her? Therefore, divide her right away, for I will have half; there is no remedy — you must do it."

"Well, before I will go back on my word to my friend, take all of her," Eumenides said. "Here, Jack, I'll give her to thee."

"Nay, neither more nor less, master," the Ghost of Jack said, "but exactly just half."

Eumenides remembered Erestus' prophecy:

"*Bestow thy alms, give more than all*"

"*Till dead men's bones come at thy call.*"

Eumenides had bestowed alms and had given almost all of his money to bury Jack, but he had not given more than all he had. But now he was being asked to give more than all the money he had had. The Ghost of Jack said that he wanted half of Delia.

But if Eumenides gave more than all he had, then dead men's bones — that is, the Ghost of Jack — would come at thy — his — call. Why would Eumenides call dead men's bones? To do good, not evil. In other words, things would work out to a good conclusion.

"Before I will falsify my faith and break my word to my friend, I will divide her," Eumenides said. "Jack, thou shall have half of Delia."

"Be not so cruel to our sister, gentle knight," the first brother said.

"Oh, spare fair Delia!" the second brother said. "She deserves no death."

"Be calm," Eumenides said. "I gave my word to him."

He then said, "Therefore prepare thyself, Delia, for thou must die."

"Then farewell, world!" Delia said. "Adieu, Eumenides!"

Delia did not run away. Her two brothers did not rush to save her. Erestus and Venelia stayed silent. Eumenides raised his sword to cleave Delia into equal halves.

Why?

They already knew there would be a happy ending. The Ghost of Jack had proven himself to be a benevolent ghost. All had been raised in a society filled with old wives who told old wives' tales. One common feature in such tales was the friendship test. The friend would be tested by being asked to live up to a promise, which turned out to involve performing a horrible task. If he was willing to perform it, he had proven that he was a man of his word and a true friend. But because the other person was also a friend, he would stop the first person from doing the horrible act.

Delia and all others present knew she was in no danger.

Eumenides raised his sword and prepared to strike Delia — and the Ghost of Jack stopped him.

He said, "Stop, master; that I have tested your faithfulness to your word is sufficient. Do you now remember when you paid for the burying of a poor fellow?"

"Aye, very well, Jack."

"Then, master, thank that good deed for this good turn, and so God be with you all!"

The Ghost of Jack leapt down into the ground.

"Jack, what, are thou gone?" Eumenides said. "Then farewell, Jack!"

He then said, "Come, brothers, and my beauteous Delia, Erestus, and thy dear Venelia. We will go to Thessaly with joyful hearts."

"Agreed," the others said. "We will follow thee and Delia."

Everyone except Frolic, Fantastic, and Madge exited.

"What, gammer, asleep?" Fantastic asked.

"By the mass, son, it is almost day; and my windows — my eyes — are shut at the cock's-crow!" Madge said. "My eyes should have been open!"

"Do you hear me, gammer?" Frolic said. "I think this Jack bore a great influence among them."

"Oh, man, this was the ghost of the poor man over whom they had such a quarrel about burying, and that caused him to help the wandering knight so much," Madge said. "But come, let us go in. We will have a cup of ale and a toast to use as a sop in it this morning, and then we will part."

"Then you have made an end of your tale, gammer?" Fantastic asked.

"Yes, indeed," Madge said. "When this was done, I took a piece of bread and cheese, and came my way; and so shall you, too, before you go, have gone to your breakfast."

Madge has told and witnessed this story many times before, and her custom, after finishing the tale, is to eat breakfast with those to whom she had told the story, and so she has invited her audience to have breakfast with her.

APPENDIX A: NOTES

— Scene 4 —

Whoo! he comes upon me with 'a superfantial substance, and the foison of the earth', that I know not what he means.

(lines 309-310 in New Mermaids edition)

(lines 338-339 in The Revels Plays edition)

Charles Whitworth wrote this:

It is just possible, however, that Peele wrote 'superstantial'; a compositor might have misread a manuscript 'st' as 'f' (especially with so many other 's's', and 'st's' and 'f's' in the immediate vicinity). Two medieval Latin philosophical terms, superstantia *and* supersubstantia, *meant, respectively, 'formally (but not physically) existent' and 'transcending substance'. Thus 'supersubstantial substance' would be clever nonsense: it would be literally self-contradictory. It would thus also continue the Latin wordplay of [lines] 272-5, and it sounds as if it means 'super-abundance', i.e. 'foison'.*

Source: Peele, George. *The Old Wife's Tale*. Ed. Charles Whitworth. New Mermaids. London: A & C Black. New York: W W Norton. 1996. P. 20.

— Scene 6 —

[...] he gave fourscore and nineteen mourning gowns to the parish when he died [...]

(lines 470-471 in New Mermaids edition)

(lines 507-508 in The Revels Plays edition)

Patricia Binnie wrote this:

No previous editor has annotated the phrase ["mourning gowns"], and I am indebted to the General Editor for finding this information: 'In 1575 Sir Thomas Gresham directed in his will that black gowns of cloth at 6s. 8d. the yard were to be given to a hundred poor men and a hundred poor women to bring him to his grave; and at Christopher Hatton's funeral in 1592 the bier was preceded by one hundred poor people whose gowns and caps were given them.' (Shakespeare's England (1916), II, p. 149)

Source: Peele, George. *The Old Wives Tale*. Ed. Patricia Binnie. The Revels Plays. Manchester, England, and Baltimore, Maryland: Manchester University Press and The Johns Hopkins Press, 1980. P. 65.

— Scene 9 —

[...] *ka, wilshaw!* [...]

(line 569 in New Mermaids edition)

(line 707 in The Revels Plays edition)

"Ka" means "quotha" or "he said."

Some ideas:

1) Possibly, "Wilshaw" is a name, or it is a play on "pshaw."

Some names are used as insults. For example, Urban Dictionary defines "Poindexter" in this way.

one who looks and acts like a nerd but does not posses [sic] the super-natural intelligence of a nerd.

Source: "poindexter." Urban Dictionary. Accessed 13 January 2019 <https://tinyurl.com/ydde8629>.

The *Oxford English Dictionary* defines "shaw" as a noun as "A thicket, a small wood, copse or grove" and as a verb as "To fence or border (a field) with a shaw." "Wil" may be derived from the obsolete Welsh word *"gwil"* meaning "tricky" or "capricious," as described below.

For what it's worth, here is some information about the name "Wilshaw" from <surnamedb.com> (Surname Database):

67

This interesting and long-established surname, with variant spellings Wilsher, Wilcher, Wilshire, Wiltshe(a)r and Wilshaw, is of Anglo-Saxon origin, and is a regional name from the county of Wiltshire in south western England. Recorded as "Wiltunscir" in the Anglo-Saxon Chronicle, dated 870, and as "Wiltescire" in the Domesday Book of 1086, the name derives from Wilton, once the principal town of the county, and the Olde English pre 7th Century "scir", a district or administrative division. Wilton, itself is named from the Olde English "tun", a settlement, and "Wil", a shorter form of the river-name "Wylye", believed to derive from the obsolete Welsh "gwil", meaning "tricky" or "capricious"; hence, "settlement on the river Wylye". The surname was first recorded in the mid 12th Century, and other early recordings include: Nicholas de Wiltesir, who appeared in the 1207 Curia Regis Rolls of Wiltshire, and Thomas Wylshere, who was recorded as a witness in the 1483 Fine Court Rolls of Cambridgeshire. On July 22nd 1543, Elizabeth Wilsher and Richard Smyth were married in Twickenham, London. A Coat of Arms granted to the family is described thus: "Per chevron blue and gold, in chief six crosses crosslet of the second. Crest - A lion rampant red maned proper." The first recorded spelling of the family name is shown to be that of Hunfr' de Wilechier, which was dated 1157, in the "Pipe Rolls of Sussex", during the reign of King Henry 11, known as "The Builder of Churches", 1154 - 1189. Surnames became necessary when governments introduced personal taxation. In England this was known as Poll Tax. Throughout the centuries, surnames in every country have continued to "develop" often leading to astonishing variants of the original spelling.

Source: "Last Name: Wilshaw." The Surname Internet Database. Accessed 9 January 2019.

<https://tinyurl.com/y7dx5umk>.

In my opinion, "wilshaw" may be a name but it is very likely a play on words, as I say in my retelling of the play. Instead of saying "pshaw," Zantippa says "wilshaw," which combines the meanings of "pshaw" and of "tricky" or *gwil*."

2) Another possibility is that "wilshaw" is the dialectical "wilta-shalta," meaning "willy-nilly." The meaning is that Huanebango chooses his words willy-nilly. The editors of *Elizabethan Plays* write in a note that "ka, wilshaw!" means this:

"*Quotha wilta-shalta, i.e., quoth he willy-nilly.*"

Source: *Elizabethan Plays*. Edited by Arthur H. Nethercot, Charles R. Baskervill, and Virgil B. Heltzel. Revised by Arthur H. Nethercot. New York: Holt, Rinehart and Winston, 1971. P. 255.

The definition for "wilta-shalta" as "willy-nilly" can be found in this book:

English Dialect Dictionary, Being Complete Vocabulary All Dialect Words Still Use, Or Known Have Been Use During Last Two Hundred Years: T-Z. Supplement. Bibliography. Grammar. Edited by Joseph Wright. Published by Henry Frowde, Amen Corner. E.C., London. 1905.

<https://tinyurl.com/y9ddyk72>.

— Scene 9 —

Stroke me smooth, and comb my head,
And thou shalt have some cockell-bread.
(lines 620-621 in New Mermaids edition)
(lines 671-672 in The Revels Plays edition)
The passage has a bawdy meaning:

If the Head is a reference to the head — and more — of a penis, then the meaning of the words "stroke me smooth" is obvious.

According to the *Oxford English Dictionary*, one meaning of "comb" as a noun is a "deep hollow or valley."

Also according to the *Oxford English Dictionary*, one meaning of "comb" as a verb is to "beat, thrash, give a 'dressing' to."

Wikipedia says this about "The 'moulding' of cocklebread" in its entry on "Cockle bread":

In the 17th century a sexual connotation is attached not to the bread itself but to "a dance that involved revealing the buttocks and simulating sexual activity" which was known as "moulding" cockle bread.[3]

John Aubrey writes of "young wenches" indulging in a "wanton sport" called "moulding of Cocklebread" where they would "get upon a Tableboard, and as they gather-up their knees and their Coates with their hands as high as they can, and then they wabble to and fro with the Buttocks as if they were kneading of Dough with their Arses".[1] While doing this, the young women would sing the rhyme:

> *My dame is sick, and gone to bed.*
> *And I'll go mould my cocklebread!*
> *Up with my heels and down with my head,*
> *And this is the way to mould cockle-bread.[4]*

Aubrey compares this, writing "I did imagine nothing to have been in this but mere wantonness of youth ... but I find in Buchardus's book Methodus Confitendi ... one of the articles of interrogating a young woman is, if she did ever subjugere panem clunibus, and then bake it, and give it to the one she loved to eat".[2] From this he decides "I find it to be a relic of natural magic, an unlawful philtrum" (i.e. aphrodisiac or love charm).[5][2]

Writing in A Dictionary of Sexual Language and Imagery in Shakespearean and Stuart Literature, *Gordon Williams sees Aubrey's "wanton sport" in a 1641 mention of moulding cocklebread, a "sexual sense" in a prayer mentioning the practice from 1683, and considers it "transparent" in the 1683 Fifteen Real Conforts Of Matrimony which "tells how 'Mrs. Betty has been Moulding of Cockle-bread, and her mother discovers it'; the consequence is a 'By-blow in her belly'".[6]*

Footnotes:

2) Hazlitt, William Carew (1905). *Faith and Folklore: a dictionary of national beliefs, superstitions and popular customs, past and current, with their classical and foreign analogues, described and illustrated.* London: Reeves and Turner. pp. 331–332. Retrieved 2014-09-19.

3) Richard Brome (25 June 2014). *A Jovial Crew.* A&C Black. p. 122. ISBN 978-1-4081-4013-0.

4) Brand, John (1854). *Observations on the Popular Antiquities of Great Britain: Chiefly Illustrating the Origin of Our Vulgar and Provincial Customs, Ceremonies, and Superstitions.* II. G. Bohn. p. 414.

5) A. McLaren, *Reproductive Rituals* (1984), p. 37.

6) Gordon Williams (13 September 2001). *A Dictionary of Sexual Language and Imagery in Shakespearean and Stuart Literature: Three Volume Set Volume I A-F Volume II G-P Volume III Q-Z.* A. & C. Black. pp. 264–265. ISBN 978-0-485-11393-8.

— Scene 10 —

are not you the man, sir, deny it if you can, sir, that came from a strange place in the land of Catita, where a Jack-an-apes flies with his tail in his mouth, to seek out a lady as white as snow and as red as blood?

(Lines 689-692 in New Mermaids edition)

(Lines 741-745 in Revels editions)

"Catita" may be a made-up word to represent a fairy-tale land, but it does have some definitions, some or all of which may be contemporary rather than Elizabethan.

In Portuguese, "*catita*" (male) means "elegant person."

In Portuguese, "*catita*" (female) means "house mouse, small sail."

Source of two definitions above:

https://en.bab.la/dictionary/portuguese-english/catita

In Latin American Spanish, "*catita*" means "parrot."

Source of above definition:

http://www.spanishdict.com/translate/catita

According to Wiktionary, *"catita"* is Portuguese (Portugal and Brazil) and can mean these things:

1) short-tailed opossum (as a noun)
2) pretty (nice-looking) (as an adjective)
Source: https://en.wiktionary.org/wiki/catita

APPENDIX B: ABOUT THE AUTHOR

It was a dark and stormy night. Suddenly a cry rang out, and on a hot summer night in 1954, Josephine, wife of Carl Bruce, gave birth to a boy — me. Unfortunately, this young married couple allowed Reuben Saturday, Josephine's brother, to name their first-born. Reuben, aka "The Joker," decided that Bruce was a nice name, so he decided to name me Bruce Bruce. I have gone by my middle name — David — ever since.

Being named Bruce David Bruce hasn't been all bad. Bank tellers remember me very quickly, so I don't often have to show an ID. It can be fun in charades, also. When I was a counselor as a teenager at Camp Echoing Hills in Warsaw, Ohio, a fellow counselor gave the signs for "sounds like" and "two words," then she pointed to a bruise on her leg twice. Bruise Bruise? Oh yeah, Bruce Bruce is the answer!

Uncle Reuben, by the way, gave me a haircut when I was in kindergarten. He cut my hair short and shaved a small bald spot on the back of my head. My mother wouldn't let me go to school until the bald spot grew out again.

Of all my brothers and sisters (six in all), I am the only transplant to Athens, Ohio. I was born in Newark, Ohio, and have lived all around Southeastern Ohio. However, I moved to Athens to go to Ohio University and have never left.

At Ohio U, I never could make up my mind whether to major in English or Philosophy, so I got a bachelor's degree with a double major in both areas, then I added a Master of Arts degree in English and a Master of Arts degree in Philosophy. Yes, I have my MAMA degree.

Currently, and for a long time to come (I eat fruits and veggies), I am spending my retirement writing books such as *Nadia Comaneci: Perfect 10*, *The Funniest People in Dance*, *Homer's* Iliad: *A Retelling in Prose*, and *William Shakespeare's* Othello: *A Retelling in Prose*.

By the way, my sister Brenda Kennedy writes romances such as A New Beginning and Shattered Dreams.

APPENDIX C: SOME BOOKS BY DAVID BRUCE

Retellings of a Classic Work of Literature

Arden of Faversham: *A Retelling*

Ben Jonson's The Alchemist: *A Retelling*

Ben Jonson's The Arraignment, or Poetaster: *A Retelling*

Ben Jonson's Bartholomew Fair: *A Retelling*

Ben Jonson's The Case is Altered: *A Retelling*

Ben Jonson's Catiline's Conspiracy: *A Retelling*

Ben Jonson's The Devil is an Ass: *A Retelling*

Ben Jonson's Epicene: *A Retelling*

Ben Jonson's Every Man in His Humor: *A Retelling*

Ben Jonson's Every Man Out of His Humor: *A Retelling*

Ben Jonson's The Fountain of Self-Love, or Cynthia's Revels: *A Retelling*

Ben Jonson's The Magnetic Lady, or Humors Reconciled: *A Retelling*

Ben Jonson's The New Inn, or The Light Heart: *A Retelling*

Ben Jonson's Sejanus' Fall: *A Retelling*

Ben Jonson's The Staple of News: *A Retelling*

Ben Jonson's A Tale of a Tub: *A Retelling*

Ben Jonson's Volpone, or the Fox: *A Retelling*

Christopher Marlowe's Complete Plays: Retellings

Christopher Marlowe's Dido, Queen of Carthage: *A Retelling*

Christopher Marlowe's Doctor Faustus: *Retellings of the 1604 A-Text and of the 1616 B-Text*

Christopher Marlowe's Edward II: *A Retelling*

Christopher Marlowe's The Massacre at Paris: *A Retelling*

Christopher Marlowe's The Rich Jew of Malta: *A Retelling*

Christopher Marlowe's Tamburlaine, Parts 1 and 2: *Retellings*

Dante's Divine Comedy: *A Retelling in Prose*

Dante's Inferno: *A Retelling in Prose*

Dante's Purgatory: *A Retelling in Prose*

Dante's Paradise: *A Retelling in Prose*

The Famous Victories of Henry V: *A Retelling*

From the Iliad *to the* Odyssey: *A Retelling in Prose of Quintus of Smyrna's* Posthomerica

George Chapman, Ben Jonson, and John Marston's Eastward Ho! *A Retelling*

George Peele's The Arraignment of Paris: *A Retelling*

George Peele's The Battle of Alcazar: *A Retelling*

George Peele's David and Bathsheba, and the Tragedy of Absalom: *A Retelling*

George Peele's Edward I: *A Retelling*

George Peele's The Old Wives' Tale: *A Retelling*

George-a-Greene: *A Retelling*

The History of King Leir: *A Retelling*

Homer's Iliad: *A Retelling in Prose*

Homer's Odyssey: *A Retelling in Prose*

J.W. Gent.'s The Valiant Scot: *A Retelling*

Jason and the Argonauts: A Retelling in Prose of Apollonius of Rhodes' Argonautica

John Ford: Eight Plays Translated into Modern English

John Ford's The Broken Heart: *A Retelling*

John Ford's The Fancies, Chaste and Noble: *A Retelling*

John Ford's The Lady's Trial: *A Retelling*

John Ford's The Lover's Melancholy: *A Retelling*

John Ford's Love's Sacrifice: *A Retelling*

John Ford's Perkin Warbeck: *A Retelling*

John Ford's The Queen: *A Retelling*

John Ford's 'Tis Pity She's a Whore: *A Retelling*

John Lyly's Campaspe: *A Retelling*

John Lyly's Endymion, The Man in the Moon: *A Retelling*

John Lyly's Galatea: *A Retelling*

John Lyly's Love's Metamorphosis: *A Retelling*

John Lyly's Midas: *A Retelling*

John Lyly's Mother Bombie: *A Retelling*

John Lyly's Sappho and Phao: *A Retelling*

John Lyly's The Woman in the Moon: *A Retelling*

John Webster's The White Devil: *A Retelling*

King Edward III: *A Retelling*

Mankind: *A Medieval Morality Play* (A Retelling)

Margaret Cavendish's The Unnatural Tragedy: *A Retelling*

The Merry Devil of Edmonton: *A Retelling*

The Summoning of Everyman: *A Medieval Morality Play* (A Retelling)

Robert Greene's Friar Bacon and Friar Bungay: *A Retelling*

The Taming of a Shrew: *A Retelling*

Tarlton's Jests: A Retelling

Thomas Middleton's A Chaste Maid in Cheapside: *A Retelling*

Thomas Middleton's Women Beware Women: *A Retelling*

Thomas Middleton and Thomas Dekker's The Roaring Girl: *A Retelling*

Thomas Middleton and William Rowley's The Changeling: *A Retelling*

The Trojan War and Its Aftermath: Four Ancient Epic Poems

Virgil's Aeneid: *A Retelling in Prose*

William Shakespeare's 5 Late Romances: Retellings in Prose

William Shakespeare's 10 Histories: Retellings in Prose

William Shakespeare's 11 Tragedies: Retellings in Prose

William Shakespeare's 12 Comedies: Retellings in Prose

William Shakespeare's 38 Plays: Retellings in Prose

William Shakespeare's 1 Henry IV, aka Henry IV, Part 1: *A Retelling in Prose*

William Shakespeare's 2 Henry IV, aka Henry IV, Part 2: *A Retelling in Prose*

William Shakespeare's 1 Henry VI, aka Henry VI, Part 1: *A Retelling in Prose*

William Shakespeare's 2 Henry VI, aka Henry VI, Part 2: *A Retelling in Prose*

William Shakespeare's 3 Henry VI, aka Henry VI, Part 3: *A Retelling in Prose*

William Shakespeare's All's Well that Ends Well: *A Retelling in Prose*

William Shakespeare's Antony and Cleopatra: *A Retelling in Prose*

William Shakespeare's As You Like It: *A Retelling in Prose*

William Shakespeare's The Comedy of Errors: *A Retelling in Prose*

William Shakespeare's Coriolanus: *A Retelling in Prose*

William Shakespeare's Cymbeline: *A Retelling in Prose*

William Shakespeare's Hamlet: *A Retelling in Prose*

William Shakespeare's Henry V: *A Retelling in Prose*

William Shakespeare's Henry VIII: *A Retelling in Prose*
William Shakespeare's Julius Caesar: *A Retelling in Prose*
William Shakespeare's King John: *A Retelling in Prose*
William Shakespeare's King Lear: *A Retelling in Prose*
William Shakespeare's Love's Labor's Lost: *A Retelling in Prose*
William Shakespeare's Macbeth: *A Retelling in Prose*
William Shakespeare's Measure for Measure: *A Retelling in Prose*
William Shakespeare's The Merchant of Venice: *A Retelling in Prose*
William Shakespeare's The Merry Wives of Windsor: *A Retelling in Prose*
William Shakespeare's A Midsummer Night's Dream: *A Retelling in Prose*
William Shakespeare's Much Ado About Nothing: *A Retelling in Prose*
William Shakespeare's Othello: *A Retelling in Prose*
William Shakespeare's Pericles, Prince of Tyre: *A Retelling in Prose*
William Shakespeare's Richard II: *A Retelling in Prose*
William Shakespeare's Richard III: *A Retelling in Prose*
William Shakespeare's Romeo and Juliet: *A Retelling in Prose*
William Shakespeare's The Taming of the Shrew: *A Retelling in Prose*
William Shakespeare's The Tempest: *A Retelling in Prose*
William Shakespeare's Timon of Athens: *A Retelling in Prose*
William Shakespeare's Titus Andronicus: *A Retelling in Prose*
William Shakespeare's Troilus and Cressida: *A Retelling in Prose*
William Shakespeare's Twelfth Night: *A Retelling in Prose*
William Shakespeare's The Two Gentlemen of Verona: *A Retelling in Prose*
William Shakespeare's The Two Noble Kinsmen: *A Retelling in Prose*

William Shakespeare's The Winter's Tale: A Retelling in Prose

www.ingramcontent.com/pod-product-compliance
Lightning Source LLC
Chambersburg PA
CBHW031401160726
47993CB00003B/1064